The River

Story by Tania Cox
Illustrations by Francesca Ficorilli

The River

Text: Tania Cox
Publishers: Tania Mazzeo and Eliza Webb
Series consultant: Amanda Sutera
Hands on Heads Consulting
Editor: Gemma Smith
Project editors: Annabel Smith and
Jarrah Moore
Designer: Jess Kelly
Project designer: Danielle Maccarone
Illustrations: Francesca Ficorilli
Production controller: Renee Tome

NovaStar

ISBN 978 0 17 033469 3

Cengage Learning Australia
Level 5, 80 Dorcas Street
Southbank VIC 3006 Australia
Phone: 1300 790 853
Email: aust.nelsonprimary@cengage.com

For learning solutions, visit **cengage.com.au**

Printed in China by 1010 Printing International Ltd
1 2 3 4 5 6 7 29 28 27 26 25

Nelson acknowledges the Traditional Owners and Custodians of the lands of all First Nations Peoples. We pay respect to Elders past and present, and extend that respect to all First Nations Peoples today.

Contents

DANGER

Chapter 1

The Discovery

The annual family camping trip at Falls River was going as smoothly as Dad's bald head. It was the weekend before the school holidays. Lots of families would be arriving soon, but for now it was peaceful. Just the way Zac, Freddy and their dad liked it.

Late on Saturday morning, Dad said, "I'm going to pick up Grandad from town. Stay close to camp and don't go into the river while I'm gone." He pointed to the nearby white sign with a red border. Its bold black words glared at Zac.

This had always been the rule. Even back when Grandad had camped at Falls River with his family as a boy.

Dad's blue ute backfired its way along the dusty red track out of the campsite.

Zac grabbed his backpack off the ground. "Freddy, let's go!"

His younger brother didn't answer. Zac looked around, but he couldn't spot him.

"Freddy!" called Zac. Where was he? They only had one hour or so before Dad returned, and Zac had a plan.

"Here!" called Freddy, from behind a big, shady gum tree. He had a stash of salami sticks and bread rolls stuffed in his backpack.

No wonder Freddy was quiet. He was eating.

Freddy used to always talk with his mouth full of food when he was younger. Then Great-Aunt Petula came for Christmas lunch a few years ago. She talked, ate and spat projectiles of food all at the same time. She got Freddy in the eyeball with a piece of chewed-up turkey! After her visit, Freddy never spoke while he was eating again.

"Quick, Freddy, let's go to the river," said Zac.

Freddy finished eating a salami stick. "But Dad and the sign both said not to go into the river. Besides, I've been looking forward to going on a nature walk all morning."

Freddy and his friends had recently formed a club called the Tree Troopers. It was all about nature for Freddy right now. Well, nature and food.

"We won't go *into* the river," said Zac. "We'll just have a closer look at it."

Freddy nodded hesitantly. He tried to zip up his backpack which was bursting with snacks. He swung it over his shoulder. "For an emergency snack attack."

Zac rolled his eyes. "Let's go!"

The brothers raced towards the river. It was noon on a steamy summer's day. It only took them a couple of minutes to get there, but they were hot and out of breath when they arrived. Zac sat down and leant back against the cool riverbank.

"Mulberries," squealed Freddy, pointing at a heavily loaded mulberry tree.

Zac laughed. "Do you think of anything other than food?"

Then something caught Zac's eye. His heart skipped a beat. He could see the wooden tip of something poking out from the big mulberry leaves. He ran over and pushed some low branches aside. "Freddy!" he shouted. "Come and see what I've found!"

There, tucked away beneath the mulberry tree, lay an old wooden canoe.

Chapter 2

The Map

Zac stared at the canoe. "So cool," he whispered. Freddy poked his head through the mulberry leaves. "Wow ... a canoe! Whose is it?"

Zac flicked thick, sticky cobwebs and layers of leaves off the canoe. "It's too old to be anyone's any more. Let's pull it out and have a better look."

The boys dragged the canoe out from under the tree and onto the slippery riverbank.

Zac knelt beside it. Two faded life jackets were crammed under the bow and a wooden oar lay in the bottom of the canoe. Underneath the oar was a shabby piece of cloth, stiff with age.

Freddy looked over Zac's shoulder. "What's that?" he asked, pointing at the old cloth.

Zac picked up the cloth. Near one edge was a drawing of a bird sitting on a canoe. Next to the bird were drawings of trees, some logs and what looked like a worm. Further along were more logs, a few trees and a fish with a long snout. Then, a faint, stripy animal appeared next to piles of logs in a treeless area. Right at the edge of the cloth were downward, curved arrows.

"It looks like some kind of map of the river," said Zac.

“What could these drawings mean?” asked Freddy.

Zac stared at the canoe. He glanced at the river. Then he stared at the canoe again. A smile crept across his face. “Freddy, are you thinking what I’m thinking?”

“You want a salami stick too?” asked Freddy, reaching into his backpack.

Zac rolled his eyes. “No! I’m thinking, let’s take the canoe on the river and find out what this map means!”

Freddy scratched his head. “But Dad and the sign said not to go into the river.”

"Technically," said Zac, "we aren't going *into* the river. We'll be floating *on top* of it in a canoe." He folded up the map and tucked it into the side pocket of his shorts.

Freddy looked down at his feet. “I guess so,” he said, slowly.

“Great! Put this on and help me push,” said Zac, tossing Freddy one of the life jackets.

Once they both had life jackets on, the boys raced around to the back of the canoe. They pushed. They shoved. But the canoe was stuck to the riverbank like gum to a school shoe.

"Push harder, Freddy!" called Zac. Then his foot slipped on the muddy riverbank. Zac fell forwards into the canoe and hit his head hard against the bottom of it.

"Ouch!" Zac's head throbbed, but his eyes widened. Staring up at him was a message carved into the bottom of the canoe.

Zac pulled himself out of the canoe. "Freddy! Stop pushing and look!" he called, pointing to the message. He read it aloud. "For a peaceful journey, keep the kookaburra quiet."

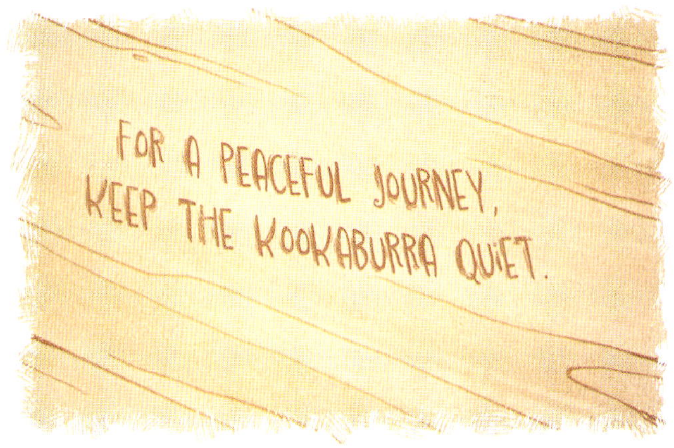

"What do you think it means?" asked Freddy, reaching into his backpack and pulling out a fresh bread roll.

Zac thought for a moment and shrugged. "Probably nothing. Let's try once more," he said, moving to the back of the canoe and pushing again. Then, as if saying those words out loud was like a password, the canoe slid smoothly into the river.

Chapter 3

The Chase

"Jump in, Freddy!" shouted Zac, scrambling into the bow of the canoe and grabbing the oar.

Freddy climbed in and sat in the back. Zac began to paddle.

Trees were snuggled together along the riverbank. They leant and arched their leafy emerald branches over the brothers as they passed underneath in the canoe. Other trees towered up to the clear blue sky. It was peaceful.

Zac stopped paddling and let the river's gentle current carry the canoe along.

Zac found himself reading the message carved into the bottom of the canoe again. *For a peaceful journey, keep the kookaburra quiet.* He pulled the map from his pocket and stared at what looked like a worm, a long-snouted fish and a stripy animal.

Thud!

Zac looked up.

Freddy spun around.

A floating log had hit the side of the canoe. Three other logs lay lifelessly among strong, tall trees on the riverbank. They looked like they'd been chopped down recently.

Just then, a kookaburra flew out from a red gum tree. It swooped over their heads and laughed. *Ooh-ooh-ah! Ooh-ooh-ah!*

Suddenly, Freddy pointed behind Zac. "Snake!" he yelled. "It came out from the trees on the riverbank!"

"It's probably just a stick," said Zac, looking back over his shoulder.

But it wasn't a stick! It was rippling through the water towards them. "Snake!" cried Zac, shoving the map back into his pocket.

"It's a Grey Snake! An endangered species!" shouted Freddy.

Zac paddled like the water was on fire. He glanced back. The hissing snake rippled along the water, coming right for them. Then the snake struck at the floating log.

"Listen, Tree Trooper, as much as I like hearing what you know about endangered animals, I'm the one feeling endangered right now!" Zac cried.

"It looks mad," said Freddy. "Maybe that log was its home before someone chopped the tree down."

The kookaburra swooped over their heads again and landed on a log on the bank. It laughed again. *Ooh-ooh-ah! Ooh-ooh-ah!*

Zac paddled the canoe furiously alongside the riverbank. There were more logs here, rather than strong, tall trees. It looked familiar. Hadn't a part of the map shown an area like this?

Splash! Splash!

Freddy let out an ear-bursting scream. He looked both scared and excited as he pointed at the water behind them.

Zac spun around.

Something that looked like a long, sharp-toothed saw emerged from the water and slashed wildly at the log.

“That’s a Largetooth Sawfish! It’s critically endangered!” cried Freddy. “I never thought I’d see one of those!”

“I wish I’d never seen one!” shouted Zac. It felt like his heart was pumping hot chilli around his body instead of blood. “I don’t think he wants to share his home with us!”

Now Zac and Freddy had a snake *and* a sawfish chasing them!

Zac tried to turn the canoe around, to go back to camp. But the current had become too strong. Instead, he paddled frantically ahead, away from the snake and sawfish.

Then, Zac’s stomach twisted into a double knot as a terrible thought about the map flickered across his mind. If what had looked like an earthworm was a snake, and the fish with the long snout was a sawfish, then what was the faintly drawn animal with the stripes?

Suddenly, from up ahead where piles of logs lay in a treeless area on the riverbank, a familiar laugh broke out. *Ooh-ooh-ah! Ooh-ooh-ah!*

Then they heard a loud GROWL!

The whole canoe shook as the guttural sound rippled through the air.

“Tiger!” cried Freddy.

Chapter 4

The Tiger and the Falls

Zac turned to see the same thing Freddy had seen: there really *was* a tiger. It had run out from behind a pile of logs on the treeless riverbank, as if it wanted to chase the canoe too.

Zac screamed so loudly that his tonsils felt ready to pop! The tiger was a ghostly shape – just like the faintly drawn animal in the treeless area on the map. Two piercing eyes glared out from its narrow head. But it wasn't like the tigers at the zoo.

"Tasmanian Tiger!" screamed Freddy. "But it can't be ... they're extinct!" Freddy didn't look excited now, just scared.

"No wonder it looks like a ghost!" yelled Zac, paddling so fast that hot pain seared up his arms.

The tiger leapt off the bank, into the water.

"It looks mad! And it's swimming after us!" cried Freddy. "I hope it doesn't think we chopped down its forest home." He curled up into a shaking, wailing ball.

The tiger kept growling and Freddy kept screaming, both noises piercing Zac's eardrums. The tiger flashed its dagger-like teeth. Behind the tiger in the river, the snake darted out its long tongue and the sawfish swung its sharp-toothed snout in the air.

"Why did I ignore the warnings?" Zac groaned.

The kookaburra swooped over Zac's head.

"Go back to your tree, you crazy kookaburra!" yelled Zac, pointing to the riverbank with the oar. But the riverbank was treeless. The kookaburra swooped over Zac's head again.

Each time the kookaburra laughs, something appears from the map, Zac thought, trembling. *Will there be another animal, fearlessly protecting its home?*

Then Zac froze. That message about the kookaburra *did* mean something. He stared at the words carved into the bottom of the canoe. *For a peaceful journey, keep the kookaburra quiet.*

But *how* to keep the kookaburra quiet?

Zac tried to think, but Freddy's screeching made it impossible. Zac paddled with aching arms. The snake, sawfish and tiger were getting closer!

What came next on the map? Zac shuddered. *Was it the downward arrows*? He couldn't remember!

Just then, the kookaburra swooped along the entire length of the canoe and let out its loudest laugh yet. *Ooh-ooh-ah-ah! Ooh-ooh-ah-ah!*

ROOOOAR! went the river. Zac's head snapped up. He knew what those arrows meant now.

"Waterfall!" yelled Zac. "Hang on, Freddy!"

Raging water tossed the canoe around like a dog with a soft toy. Zac's breakfast triple somersaulted in his stomach. He was sure the animals were trying to chase the canoe out of their home, right over the edge of the waterfall.

The kookaburra swooped over the brothers once again.

Zac paddled furiously towards the shore, but the current was too strong and he couldn't make any headway. Freddy's shrieks became hysterical. How could Zac think of a way to keep the kookaburra quiet with Freddy shrieking, the tiger growling and the waterfall roaring?

"Freddy! We need to think our way out of this, not scream! Stuff some food in your mouth and keep quiet!" yelled Zac.

Then he stopped paddling. His eyes raced along the bottom of the canoe again. *For a peaceful journey, keep the kookaburra quiet.*

"That's it!" cried Zac, dropping the oar inside the canoe.

Zac grabbed Freddy's backpack and pulled out a bread roll. "I hope the kookaburra believes in eating quietly, like you do, Freddy!"

Zac tossed the roll up to the laughing kookaburra as it swooped overhead.

The bread roll flipped over and over, crumbs scattering below.

The kookaburra snatched the roll out of the air.

Suddenly, all went quiet.

Chapter 5

The Surprise

Whoosh! The kookaburra swooped towards the bank with its crusty treasure. Its beak was too full to laugh any more. It flew off along the riverbank until it found a red gum branch to land on.

Zac's eyes scanned the river. Snake, sawfish, tiger and waterfall had all disappeared. He rubbed his eyes.

Freddy was crouched sobbing in the back of the canoe.

Zac gave Freddy a gentle nudge. "Sit up, Freddy," he said. "Take a look around."

Freddy sat up like he was balancing a glass of water on his head. He looked around and cried, "The waterfall's gone! The animals have gone too! But, Zac, are we where I think we are?"

Zac nodded. "We're back on the riverbank where we found the canoe. Look, there's the mulberry tree it was under."

Zac stared at the message carved into the bottom of the canoe. *For a peaceful journey, keep the kookaburra quiet.*

A shiver ran up and down Zac's spine. "Let's go before the kookaburra laughs again." He pulled the map out of his pocket and shoved it under the oar in the bottom of the canoe.

Freddy nodded. "Should we tell anyone about this?" he asked uncertainly.

Zac's heart was still racing. "I think we should talk to Grandad first. After all, he's been coming here forever."

That night after dinner, Zac and Freddy sat around the campfire with Grandad. Dad was inspecting the dinner dishes that Zac and Freddy had quickly washed up.

Zac wasn't sure how to talk to Grandad about what had happened that afternoon. He picked up a stick and drew a sawfish in the dirt while he thought.

Grandad pointed to Zac's drawing of the sawfish. "When I was your age, the river was filled with Largetooth Sawfish like that. And when my dad, your great-grandfather, was your age, there were even Tasmanian Tigers in these forests!"

Zac looked at Freddy.

Freddy looked at Zac.

"There was a lot more forest back then," Grandad continued. "These days, there are dams, farms, houses and roads here, where the forest used to be."

Zac sighed. Which animal would disappear next, as the trees disappeared, and with them its home? *I have to help them*, he thought, drawing trees in the dirt. If only helping the animals was as easy as drawing trees back onto the riverbank with a stick.

Suddenly, Zac had an idea. He couldn't draw trees back on the riverbank, but he could put them back another way! "Grandad, I want to plant a tree whenever I come camping, to help stop more animals losing their homes. I can bring my friends to help!"

"Great idea!" said Freddy. "I can bring the Tree Troopers to help, too!"

"I'm sure my bowling buddies would come and plant some trees as well!" said Grandad, smiling.

Zac got up to put his stick in the fire. "Grandad," he said. "When you were our age, did you go into the river by yourself?"

Grandad took a deep breath and leaned towards the boys. "Just once," he said. "But technically, I didn't go *into* the river. I only floated *on top* of it, in a canoe ..."